PIONEERING
FROZEN
WORLDS

FOR ROBERT FORRO, WHOSE WONDERFUL HOUSE KEEPS ME WARM AND SNUG WHEN IT'S COLD OUTSIDE.

ACKNOWLEDGMENTS

The author would like to thank the following persons for sharing their expertise and enthusiasm: Antarctic Support Associates, Neal Brown (University of Alaska), Jim Osborn (Carnegie Mellon), Tony Gow (Cold Regions Research & Engineering Laboratory), Dr. Murray Hamlet (U.S. Army), Langdon Quetin (Marine Science Institute, University of California at Berkeley), Mark Meier (Chief of Glaciology Program, University of Colorado), Dale Andersen (NASA—Ames), Frank Salisbury (Utah State University), Ian Stirling, Wayne Z. Trivelpiece, and Susan Trivelpiece (Montana State University), Keith von der Heydt (Woods Hole Oceanographic Institution), and Dr. Gerald H. Krockover (Purdue University). The author wishes to thank the National Science Foundation for supporting her exploration of Antarctica.

PHOTO CREDITS

p. 1: Keith von der Heydt, Woods Hole Oceanographic Institution; **p. 3:** James Sweitzer; **p. 4:** National Science Foundation; **p. 5:** Mark Meier; **p. 6:** National Science Foundation; **p. 7:** James Sweitzer; **p. 8:** Arthur DeVries; **p. 9:** Laura Dishneau /Antarctic Support Associates; **p. 10 :** NASA; **p. 11:** United States Coast Guard; **p. 12:** Rubin Sheinberg; **p. 13:** United States Navy; **p. 14:** United States Navy; **p. 15:** Laura Dishneau/Antarctic Support Associates; **p. 16:** Murray Hamlet; **p. 17:** Rob McDonald, Atlanta; **p. 18:** National Science Foundation; Weatherhaven® Shelters; **p. 19:** Ian Stirling; **p. 20:** David Bubenheim/NASA; **p. 21 (left):** NASA; **(right):** Neal B. Brown; **p. 23:** Keith von der Heydt, Woods Hole Oceanographic Institution; **p. 24:** Rob McDonald, Atlanta; **p. 25:** Ian Stirling; **p. 26:** Richard Williams/United States Geologic Survey; **p. 27:** Rob McDonald, Atlanta; **p. 29:** Mark Meier; **p. 30:** Richard Williams/United States Geologic Survey; **p. 31:** Tony Gow, CRREL; **p. 32 (top):** National Science Foundation; **(bottom):** Ken Abbott, Colorado University—Boulder; **p. 33:** International Ice Patrol; **p. 34:** International Ice Patrol; **p. 35:** Rob McDonald, Atlanta; **p. 36 (top):** Dale Andersen; **(bottom):** Jim Osborn, Carnegie Mellon; **p. 38:** Langdon Quetin and Robin Ross; **p. 39:** Langdon Quetin and Robin Ross; **p. 40:** Wayne and Susan Trivelpiece, Montana State University; **p. 41:** Wayne and Susan Trivelpiece, Montana State University; **p. 42:** Arthur DeVries; **p. 43:** Rob McDonald, Atlanta; **p. 44:** Frank Salisbury; **p. 45:** Laura Dishneau/Antarctic Support Associates; **p. 46:** Juan Batista Silva, Coronel de Aviacion, Jefe De La Division Antartica; **p. 47:** Joan Kai Chan/James Sweitzer.

Atheneum Books for Young Readers
An imprint of Simon & Schuster Children's Publishing Division
1230 Avenue of the Americas
New York, New York 10020

Book design by PIXEL PRESS

The text of this book is set in 12 point Plantin

Printed in Hong Kong

First Edition

10 9 8 7 6 5 4 3 2 1

Library of Congress Cataloging-in-Publication Data
Markle, Sandra.
   Pioneering frozen worlds / by Sandra Markle. — 1st ed.
    p. cm.
   Summary: Uses simple science activities to illustrate the differences between the two polar regions, the Arctic and the Antarctic, and the problems inherent in the exploration of both.
Includes index.
   ISBN 0-689-31824-3 (cloth)
   1. Polar regions—Juvenile literature. [1. Polar regions.] I. Title.
G587.M37 1996
919.8—dc20
95-15971
CIP
AC

PIONEERING
FROZEN
WORLDS

SANDRA MARKLE

ATHENEUM BOOKS FOR YOUNG READERS

Into Frozen Worlds

From these pictures, you can tell that it isn't easy to explore and investigate frozen regions. While there are smaller frozen areas high up on mountains, it's Earth's two large frozen polar areas, the Arctic in the North and the Antarctic in the South, that especially attract explorers and scientists.

First, it's important to understand a major difference between the two regions. The Arctic is water surrounded by land while Antarctica is land, a continent, surrounded by water. Native peoples, such as the Lapps and the Inuit, have lived in the Arctic since ancient times. But no known exploration of the Antarctic took place until Captain James Cook sailed there in the 1770s. Even with the help of modern technology, Antarctica remains one of the Earth's most challenging regions. With a permanent ice cap about 3 meters (9.8 feet) thick, investigating the Arctic isn't easy either.

So how are scientists exploring Earth's frozen frontiers? What are they discovering, and how are the discoveries that are being made proving useful?

Just working and living in the Arctic and the Antarctic is a challenge. It's dark throughout the winter months. And even during the summer when the sun shines, it's cold. Winds make it even colder. Antarctica has some of the strongest winds in the world, blowing at speeds as great as 320 kilometers per hour (200 miles per hour).

Come join in the adventure, and along the way perform investigations that will let you see what it's like to be a scientist exploring the Arctic or the Antarctic. But first get ready to explore by finding out more about what these polar frontiers are like.

5

DISCOVER WHY THE POLES ARE SO COLD

First, go in a dark room, stand about 1.5 meters (5 feet) from a wall, aim a flashlight straight at the wall, and switch it on. See what a small, bright spot of light this makes. Then tip the flashlight slowly and watch the spot grow bigger and the light less intense. The sun's rays strike Earth most intensely at the equator. The Arctic and the Antarctic, the regions at the North and South Poles, receive less direct sunlight. Because of this, these regions are never warm enough to completely melt away the ice and snow.

Next, check the air temperature during the day and at night after it has been dark for two hours. Usually, the temperature is colder after dark. And that's another reason the Arctic and the Antarctic are so cold. These regions have long months of darkness. This happens because

*Even though it was summer in Antarctica, the moisture in this man's breath
quickly froze in the cold air, coating his beard with frost.*

Earth is tilted as it orbits the sun. For part of the year, Earth's North Pole is aimed toward the sun. Then the sun circles the horizon without setting. During this time, though, the South Pole is aimed away from the sun and it's dark. Now you also know why it's summer in the Arctic while it's winter in the Antarctic.

To discover yet another reason the Arctic and the Antarctic are so cold, fill a metal cake pan nearly full of water and leave it in the freezer. The next time it's warm and sunny, take this pan of ice outdoors. Hold your hand, palm down, over the ground away from the ice. Then move your hand so it's about 2.5 centimeters (1 inch) above the ice. Feel the difference? Cold radiating from the ice in the Arctic and the Antarctic help chill these regions.

Look at the penguins. Are you in the Arctic or the Antarctic? (Clue: Check solution number 8.)

HOW'S YOUR POLAR I.Q.?

You may think of the Arctic and the Antarctic as being much alike, but when you take this quiz you'll discover some important differences. Then read on to check yourself. Be careful because one of these questions may fool you.

1. You're surrounded by three-fourths of the world's fresh water, but you have to melt some to get a drink. Are you in the Arctic or the Antarctic?

2. You visit East Base, the world's most remote museum. Are you in the Arctic or the Antarctic?

3. The biggest land animal that lives there permanently is only 3 millimeters (1/10 inch) long. Are you in the Arctic or the Antarctic?

4. You visit a native Inuit family's home. Are you in the Arctic or the Antarctic?

5. Only 12 centimeters (5 inches) of new snow fell this year. Are you in the Arctic or the Antarctic?

6. It's January and it's daylight at midnight. Are you in the Arctic or the Antarctic?

7. You're going under the pole in a nuclear submarine. Are you in the Arctic or the Antarctic?

8. You've just spotted a polar bear eating a penguin. Are you in the Arctic or the Antarctic?

Solutions

1. The Antarctic. Since all this fresh water is frozen, getting a drink can require some effort. Early in the summer before the glaciers begin to melt, some research camps obtain fresh water by piling snow on top of the hut that is their living quarters. The sun and heat from inside the hut melt the snow. Then it runs into eaves and is channeled through pipes to a storage tank. Later in the summer, melting glaciers feed icy freshwater streams. In the picture, you can see snow being loaded into a machine that will melt it. This is the way McMurdo Station maintains a steady supply of fresh water.

2. East Base was originally established in 1940 when Admiral Richard Byrd led an expedition to Antarctica. It was abandoned during World War II and then reused in 1947 by a private expedition headed by a man named Finn Ronne. This team included two women, his wife and the wife of his chief pilot. They were the first women to spend the winter in Antarctica. In 1989, the Antarctic Treaty nations dedicated East Base as a museum.

3. The Antarctic. Although there are penguins and seals on this southernmost continent, these animals are only seasonal visitors. The biggest animal that is a permanent resident is a type of fly called a midge.

4. The Arctic. The Inuit are one of a number of native groups living in the extreme North. There is no native human population on Antarctica.

5. You could be in either the Arctic or the Antarctic. You might think for all the snow and ice that the Poles get a lot of precipitation, but that's not true. The average snowfall per year in Antarctica is about 12 centimeters (5 inches). The average annual precipitation in some parts of the Arctic is less than most of the Sahara Desert. The reason there's so much ice and snow in the polar regions is that most of the snow that piles up doesn't melt.

6. The Antarctic. Both Poles have a summer season when it is light during both day and night. These seasons are opposite, though, so in January it's winter in the Arctic, and summer in the Antarctic.

7. The Arctic. Remember, the Arctic is water surrounded by land while Antarctica is a continent surrounded by water. The average thickness of the Arctic's permanent ice cap is about 3 meters (9.8 feet).

8. This isn't possible. Certain animals are found only in the Arctic, others only in the Antarctic. Polar bears live in the Arctic. Most types of penguins visit in the Antarctic; none in the Arctic.

DOES ANTARCTICA CHANGE SIZE?

Look at these summer and winter satellite views of Antarctica. You can see that this frozen region gets bigger during the winter when ice builds up around it. During the summer, Antarctica is about the size of the United States and Mexico combined. In the winter, though, its area almost doubles. To get an idea of the thickness of the ice covering Antarctica, find a picture of the Eiffel Tower in Paris. Then picture eighteen Eiffel Towers stacked one on top of the other. The ice in Antarctica is a little thicker than that—as much as 4.8 kilometers (3 miles) thick. Now, find out the height of a local landmark and use it to compare the thickness of the Antarctic ice cover. Or come up with a comparison of your own.

WINTER

SUMMER

The West Antarctic ice sheet is the last place on Earth where the ocean is frozen completely from surface to sea bottom.

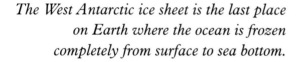

CHECK OUT RECORD COLD

To discover how cold it can get on Antarctica, try this. Put an indoor-outdoor thermometer in the freezer section of your refrigerator. After five minutes, check the temperature. The coldest temperature ever recorded on Antarctica was $-88.27^{\circ}C$ ($-126.9^{\circ}F$) on August 29, 1960. How much warmer was it inside the freezer than in Antarctica? Average winter temperatures, though, are only likely to range between $-20^{\circ}C$ ($-4^{\circ}F$) to $-30^{\circ}C$ ($-22^{\circ}F$) on different parts of the Antarctic continent and $-43^{\circ}C$ ($-45.4^{\circ}F$) in the Arctic. How much warmer or colder are those temperatures than your freezer?

How Is Technology Helping Scientists Explore?

THEY'RE BREAKING A PATH THROUGH THE ICE

Polar class icebreakers, like the one in this photo, are designed to cut a path through sea ice. Wonder how an icebreaker breaks ice? First of all the shape of its bow helps. Unlike the front of most ships, an icebreaker's bow is sloped to let the ship ride up onto the ice. Some are coated with a special Teflon-like plastic to let the ship slide more easily. Norwegian and Finnish icebreakers have water flowing down the bow to help the ship slip over the ice. But the ship doesn't just slide over the ice pack

like a sled. Three big engines blast air over the ship's propellers, making them spin fast and giving a polar class icebreaker as much as twice the horsepower of an average ship. This extra power rams the icebreaker onto the sea ice. Then the ship's massive weight smashes down, compressing and bending the ice until it cracks.

To keep the ice from punching a hole in the ship, an icebreaker's hull has strong supporting ribs. Canadian icebreakers usually have a double hull for extra protection. An icebreaker's propellers are also constructed to be especially strong —strong enough to withstand the huge chunks of ice that slip under the ship and smack into the spinning blades.

If you've ever been on a ship and felt ill as it rocked in the waves, you won't want to travel on a polar class icebreaker. Most ships have fins to help keep them steady, but fins would quickly be damaged by the ice. Icebreakers tend to be football shaped and roll with the waves.

BREAK SOME ICE

See for yourself why it's more efficient for an icebreaker to ride up onto the ice than simply shove into it. First, you'll need to freeze what will be your model sea ice, so pour water into a metal bread pan until it's about 5 centimeters (2 inches) thick. Put the pan in the freezer. When the water is frozen, set the pan in warm water in the sink for just a moment to loosen the ice block. Then slip the ice into a large plastic storage bag and set this inside a larger rectangular metal pan. Be sure you have an adult's permission and wear safety goggles for extra protection.

Now take a hammer, reach inside the bag, and press the metal head hard against the end of the ice block. Next, slide the head of the hammer up onto the ice block, lift it as much as you can inside the bag, and slam it down. Which method made it easier to break up the ice?

Can you think of a way that an icebreaker's design might be changed to help it break through sea ice even more easily? Brainstorm, listing all your ideas. Limit yourself to ten minutes to keep moving along. Then evaluate your list. Draw a diagram of the design you think is the most likely to be an improvement, explaining how it would work.

Does the flat bow of this Swedish icebreaker look odd? This innovative design helps the ship break through the ice, but it makes it harder for the ship to maneuver in open water.

The USS Pargo *has broken through the ice to allow scientists to set up experiments.*

THEY'RE DIVING UNDER THE ARCTIC ICE

Imagine diving under the Arctic ice cap to find out what's down there! That's been the dream of scientists since the USS *Nautilus* first crossed under the Arctic ice cap in 1958. Until recently, though, nuclear submarine action was limited to military operations. Then the end of the cold war made it possible for the U. S. Navy to change its policy. During the summer of 1993, the nuclear submarine USS *Pargo* carried scientists on what was the United States's first strictly scientific exploration under the Arctic ice cap.

The cruise, which took the scientists from Groton, Connecticut, to Bergen, Nor-

way, focused on the central Arctic Ocean. This region is permanently covered by ice that averages 3 meters (9.8 feet) thick. The ice is constantly in motion, moved about by surface currents and winds. It also varies in thickness in different regions as it builds up and melts, or broken pieces pack together and are reformed. One thing scientists wanted to determine was the total volume of ice. This volume will act as a baseline to check if the amount of ice decreases in the years to come. Scientists believe a decrease in the volume of ice covering the Arctic will be proof that

13

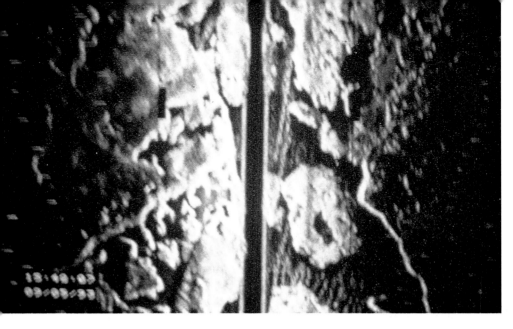

This image of the bottom surface of the ice was created when the Pargo's *sonar bounced sound waves off the ice.*

Earth's overall climate is warming up. To study the ice, the sub's upward-looking sonar, which is normally used to keep the ship from bumping into underwater ice ridges, was used to trace a profile of the bottom of the ice. At the same time, instruments aboard a satellite collected images of the surface of the ice.

Twice the USS *Pargo* surfaced through a temporary opening in the ice pack so scientists could attach special Polar Oceanographic Profiling (POP) buoys to the ice. A string of sensors hanging below the POP buoy records water temperature and salinity, or saltiness, at six depths: 10, 40, 70, 120, 200, and 300 meters (33, 131, 230, 394, 656.20, and 984 feet). The POP buoys also measure air temperature and pressure and transmit all this information to scientists via satellite. These buoys are expected to remain in the ice for up to three years, letting researchers monitor seasonal changes.

In other studies, scientists recorded the temperature and salinity of the water at different depths each time the sub surfaced. Special instruments mounted on the submarine continuously recorded temperature, salinity, and depth when the sub was submerged. Researchers collected numerous water samples to analyze once they were back on shore. Trace elements, such as Cesium-137 that enters the Atlantic from the nuclear fuel reprocessing plant located on the Irish Sea, make it possible to trace where some water goes after it leaves the Irish Sea. So the samples could be used to determine how the water flowed away from the Irish Sea, where it went, and how long it took to travel to the place where it was collected.

Plans are already under way for a second cruise under the Arctic Ocean in the near future. One day, scientists hope to have a submarine dedicated exclusively to research. Then what was once space for weapons on the sub can be converted into a deep-sea laboratory.

THEY'RE DRESSING FOR THE COLD

Besides being uncomfortable, being exposed to extremely cold air or water can damage skin. If the body's core temperature drops below 27°C (80°F), being cold can be life threatening. So anyone venturing into a cold environment needs protective clothing, and clothes need to be piled on in layers that can be shed to prevent overheating. If sweating makes clothing damp, it can give the wearer chills. The following are dressing instructions suggested by the *Field Manual for the U.S. Antarctic Program.*

Start with long underwear. This should be snug-fitting and made of a material that will repel water, drawing perspiration away from the skin.

Next, add a shirt or sweater and trousers. These clothes need to be made of a material, such as special synthetics or wool, that will continue to transport perspiration away from underwear to the environment. The fit is also important. This layer needs to trap and conserve body heat.

A layer of insulation goes over sweaters and pants. This layer should be thick, such as a jacket and trousers filled with fluffy synthetic fibers.

Finally, a windshell or an additional jacket and trousers made of water-repellent, breathable material tops the other layers. This shell permits perspiration to escape to the surface and be evaporated.

Hands and feet need special protection. First, cover hands with lightweight wool/nylon-blend gloves. Next, put on a mitten shell or leather gloves. Cover feet with

Here's a look at what's needed to be dressed for the cold.

socks and then boots. Normally, bunny boots, as they're called, provide enough protection. Bunny boots are rubber boots with an air bladder innersole to insulate feet from the cold surface below. For super-cold weather, though, there are boots made up of three insulating layers of wool fleece sealed within an outer and inner layer of rubber.

Since nearly 50 percent of the heat a person loses is radiated from the head, proper headgear is especially important. First, cover the head with a stretchy cap that has earflaps. Next, add a second cap with pull-down earflaps. In really cold weather, start with a pull-on mask that covers the face—all but the eyes—and finish with a fur-edged hood. Shield eyes with sunglasses or special goggles.

Sometimes, though, even being dressed for the cold isn't enough. Dr. Murray Hamlet, U.S. Army expert on the dangers of cold environments, suggests this emergency care for someone suspected of suffering from hypothermia or general body cooling.

1. Get the person into a shelter and out of the wind.

2. Provide dry, insulating clothing.

3. Give the person warm, sweet liquid to drink. Prepare this drink by mixing three tablespoons of sugar into warm (not hot) water. The sugar will provide quick energy to help the person generate body heat.

4. Apply heat to both sides of the person's body even if it's only the body heat of rescuers.

This person is wearing a cold water survival suit. Like a diver's wet suit, it's designed to trap and conserve body heat. Unlike a wet suit, it's loose-fitting and easy to slip on in an emergency.

HOW DOES BEING COLD AFFECT YOUR COORDINATION?

Dr. Murray Hamlet suggests trying this to see how cold affects you. First, you must check with a parent or guardian to be sure this activity is safe for you. It's not advised for anyone who may have any sort of heart condition.

Fill a sink or container two-thirds full of cold water and add four cups of crushed ice or three dozen ice cubes. Set up a task to perform while your hands are still warm. For example, try picking up something small like grains of rice. Try threading a needle. Or print your name as neatly as you can on a piece of paper.

Next, plunge your hand and forearm into the cold water. Leave it immersed long enough to count to twenty if you can stand it. If you feel any pain, immediately take your arm out of the water. As soon as you remove your arm, perform the task again.

Do your fingers feel as flexible as they did when they were warm? Is it as easy to bend your fingers and grip objects? If you print your name, does your handwriting look any different?

In cold environments, people usually wear mittens instead of gloves. Can you figure out why? (Clue: Put a glove on one hand and a mitten on the other. Think about which does a better job of trapping your body heat.) Special mittens designed for cold climate activities have a separate index finger as well as a separate thumb. Why do you suppose this design is helpful? (Clue: Try picking up something while wearing a mitten.)

THEY'RE BUILDING SHELTERS

Bases such as McMurdo in Antarctica are small towns with many of the comforts of home. Many researchers in both the Antarctic and the Arctic need to work in areas away from such permanent stations, though. For over eighty years, the standard shelter has been a two-person, teepee-style tent called the Scott polar tent. Now, technological advances have provided other easy-to-set-up shelters for camping in rugged, frozen terrain.

This Weatherhaven® shelter has a frame of curved metal tubes that slip easily into anchors. The frame is covered by vinyl-coated nylon.

18

THEY'RE TRACKING POLAR BEARS WITH SATELLITES

It's Tuesday. Do you know where polar bear number 72 is? Ian Stirling, who monitors polar bear travels by satellite, soon will. This is the day the special transmitter collar on bear number 72 is scheduled to switch on and stay on for about eight hours. Sometime during that period, the satellite will pick up the collar's signal and record the latitude and longitude of that bear's location. Then the transmitter will switch off for five more days. At the end of the month, Stirling will receive a printout showing where bear 72 and all the other bears in his study were on each check-in day.

Besides learning where they travel, Stirling has discovered a number of other traits about polar bears by tracking them. First, he's learned that bears seem to have good memories. A bear that has discovered a beached whale carcass is likely to return to that site as much as a year later. Females tend to return to the location where they were born to have their own cubs. And polar bears repeat their travels seasonally, returning to the same location each summer and each winter over the years. Stirling hopes to discover if these seasonal patterns are similar to those followed by the bear's mother. More years of tracking polar bear movements may let him find out.

Ian Stirling is holding the radio collar just removed from this tranquilized bear. The bear wore the collar for a year while Stirling tracked its travels.

One day a special indoor garden like this may supply food for colonists on the moon.

THEY'RE TESTING SPACE FARMS

A lunar colony's farm will have to be self-contained, heated to just the right temperature, and supplied with water and nutrients. What better place on Earth to set up and study a prototype space farm than Antarctica during the nine-month dark period? Even the crew wintering over is much like a space colony. The people are isolated from the world and can benefit from working with plants and eating fresh food.

Just like a space colony, the South Pole Station's farm is sealed from the environment on the top, bottom, and sides. High-intensity lamps similar to those that illuminate parking lots provide the plants with the light they need to grow. If you've ever held your hand close to (but not touching) a lamp that's been on for some time, you know that lights radiate heat as well as light. These lamps are the South Pole farm's main heat source. Additional heat—enough

to keep the air temperature about 25 °C (77 °F)—is furnished by the waste heat produced by the station's electric generators. A well-oxygenated liquid flowing over the plants' roots supplies necessary nutrients. The plants themselves help keep the air damp by giving off moisture from their leaves. This moisture is captured when it condenses on the cool walls—chilled by the ice-cold air outside—and recycled. The farm could produce anything, but right now the crops are lettuce, tomatoes, cucumbers, and zucchini.

By the year 2000, the National Science Foundation will have built a new South Pole Station on Antarctica. Then there will be another Controlled Ecological Life Support System besides the farm—a park. While it will be only about the size of two average-size living rooms put together, it will be a place where people can relax and forget the alien world outside.

What Are They Exploring in Frozen Worlds?

Wonder why researchers would eagerly travel long distances to reach very cold places? The answer is that these regions hold clues to Earth's past and future environments. The frozen parts of the planet also have the clearest skies for studying the stars. And the harsh climate and rugged terrain make it a good place to test instruments that may be used to explore the moon or Mars. Read on to discover just a few of the many exciting investigations going on in the cold.

THEY'RE INVESTIGATING THE AURORA

Compare this view of an aurora as seen from the space shuttle to the view of an aurora as seen from Earth's surface. How do you think it could be useful for researchers to be able to examine this phenomena these two different ways?

Auroras are called *aurora borealis* in the Northern Hemisphere and *aurora australis* in the Southern Hemisphere, but they are exactly the same thing. These northern and southern lights appear when solar wind, the electrically charged atoms and electrons that stream through space from the sun,

SHUTTLE VIEW

EARTH VIEW

PUT AURORA POWER TO WORK

Scientists have considered the possibility of harnessing the auroras as an energy source. They're especially interested because, unlike coal and oil, the aurora's energy supply is constantly being renewed. The technology to collect this energy supply, though, doesn't currently exist.

Brainstorm. List as many ways as you can think of that the energy producing the auroras could be collected. If you need an idea to get you started, Neal Brown, a scientist who studies the auroras, suggested a network of satellites with a means to pick up this energy and then direct it to a receiving station on Earth. To keep moving along, allow yourself only ten minutes to brainstorm. Then analyze your ideas, considering which is the most likely to be successful. You may want to visit the library and read more about auroras.

Draw a diagram of your plan and write a brief description of how it would work. Save this idea in a journal you can refer back to and reconsider as your knowledge and skills grow and as new technology becomes available.

collides with atoms of oxygen, nitrogen, and other gases high in Earth's atmosphere. This causes a reaction within the atoms of oxygen and other gases that emit energy in the form of light. Then this energy cascades down through the atmosphere, passed from molecule to molecule and atom to atom, something like a nuclear reaction.

The red color at the top of the aurora seen from space is emitted by oxygen atoms about 320 to 480 kilometers (200 to 300 miles) above Earth. Lower—about 97 to 129 kilometers (60 to 80 miles) above Earth— the chemistry of the atmosphere is different, and so the reaction that happens inside the oxygen atoms is slightly different. At this level oxygen atoms emit green light. Blue light is emitted by nitrogen.

Auroras start about 1,100 kilometers (700 miles) below each of Earth's magnetic poles and encircle Earth like a crown of light about 160 kilometers (100 miles) wide. Auroras occur twenty-four hours a day, every day, but they can't be seen easily during bright sunlight or moonlight.

Some scientists are interested in studying auroras just because they are intriguing. Others are interested because the charged particles that cause the aurora interfere with radio and satellite communications. Early in 1994, for example, two Canadian communication satellites quit working, and scientists believe they were the victims of an especially intense barrage of solar particles that caused vivid auroras. Solar particles are also blamed for surges in power lines, such as the one in 1989 that temporarily put Hydro-Quebec out of service. By better understanding auroras, researchers will be able to design communication and power equipment that is less likely to be affected by these atmospheric disturbances.

22

THEY'RE RIDING ICE FLOES
TO STUDY SEA ICE

How can an icebreaker's design be improved to take better advantage of the way ice fractures? How can ocean oil drilling platforms be built to withstand being struck by large chunks of rock-hard sea ice? How can submarines tell the sounds produced by other subs from the noise made by sea ice cracking? To be able to answer these questions and more, researchers need to understand the basic mechanics of sea ice—what kinds of stresses are likely to cause it to crack, how the ice breaks apart, and what kinds of noises it makes as it cracks or rubs and bumps against other chunks of ice. Some things can be learned about sea ice through simulations set up in a laboratory, but much more can be discovered by observing sea ice firsthand. So scientists have periodically set up camp on a chunk of sea ice about the size of a small island and used this as a floating research vessel.

So far, most of the sea ice camps have been in the Arctic. In the Antarctic, the sea ice gradually drifts north to warmer waters and melts. In the Arctic, though, the sea ice is trapped by the surrounding land and can't easily migrate south to melt. For that

This camp is situated on an ice floe being carried along by the Transpolar Drift, a current that flows from Siberia to Greenland. The ice is moving so slowly that this motion is seldom noticeable. Every now and then, though, as you can see in this picture, the ice cracks dangerously close to camp.

reason, sea ice that forms in the Arctic is likely to remain for several years or even longer. There's also more human activity for the ice to interfere with in the Arctic.

While they're camping on the ice, some scientists study the ice itself, examining its structure. Others drill holes through the ice to lower instruments into the ocean. Remotely Operated Vehicles (ROVs) let researchers view and map the underside of the ice. A special instrument lets them check the water temperature, salinity, and pressure at different depths. Still other scientists set up strain gauges to measure stress levels in the ice and arrays of special instruments that detect sounds and move-ment. Then computers process the data from all these instruments. By analyzing what causes the ice to crack and what happens when it does crack, scientists hope to learn enough to predict where a major crack is likely to occur. Then they want to be at that site to actually observe and measure what happens as the ice breaks apart.

Of course, while this research provides new clues about the properties of ice, it also makes scientists think of new questions. For example, exactly how much pressure does it take for ice of a specific thickness to crack? Or how well might ice pack behavior be predicted based on measurements received from planes and satellites?

HOW DO SEA ICE AND WATER INTERACT?

To find out, try this activity. Mix water with blue food coloring, pour it into two ice cube trays, and freeze. Fill an aquarium or clear plastic storage box half full of cold tap water. Place an indoor/outdoor thermometer underwater on the bottom of the container, wait five minutes, and then check and write down the temperature. Next, dump in the colored cubes.

Look through the side of the container. What evidence, if any, do you see that the ice is interacting with the water? Place the thermometer on the bottom of the container again. Wait five minutes and check the temperature. Is the water temperature higher, lower, or the same as it was before you added the ice?

Wiggle your hand in the water to create waves. Think of at least three words that describe the sounds you hear as the ice bumps together. Imagine how much louder big chunks of sea ice would be!

Keith von der Heydt says, "Sometimes ridges of ice squeal as they rub together. They can also make twangs and loud noises that sound like gunshots."

Young polar bears travel with their mother for about two and a half years, learning to find food for themselves.

JOIN AN ICE FLOE EXPEDITION

Imagine that you are part of an ice floe expedition. Where do you suppose you'd get fresh water to drink?

Did you figure out that you could chip out some of the ice and melt it to get fresh water? When sea ice forms, some of the salt is left behind in the ocean. Then as the ice ages, more of the brine, or very salty water, drains down through the ice, leaving the surface ice nearly salt free.

Garbage is always hauled as far from an ice floe camp as possible. Can you guess why?

Keith von der Heydt, who has been on a number of sea ice expeditions, reports, "Garbage attracts polar bears. We even had one bear stroll right up to the mess tent while we were inside having dinner."

Start a journal and write a week's accounts of your experiences on the ice floe. You may want to include a visit from a polar bear.

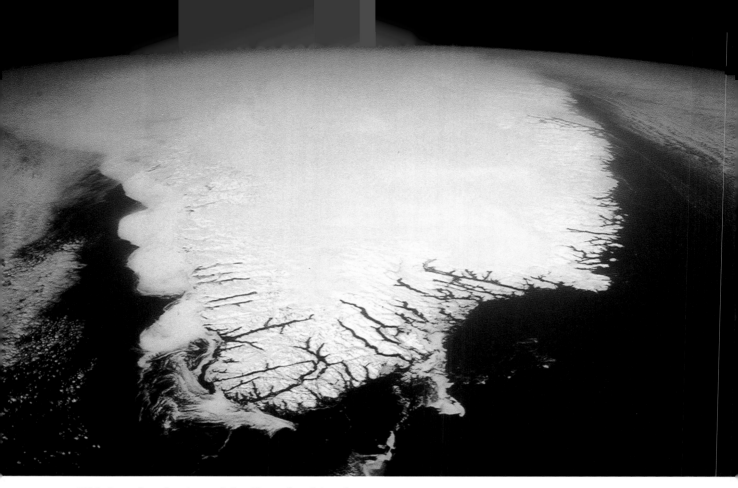

This is a shuttle view of the Greenland ice sheet.

THEY'RE INVESTIGATING GLACIERS

A glacier is a large mass of ice that originates on land. It is formed as snow piles on top of old snow, compacting it. Slowly, over many years, this ice builds up. As a rule, to be classified as a glacier, the ice must cover an area larger than one-tenth of a square kilometer (25 acres) and be more than a year old. Besides the massive ice sheets covering Greenland and Antarctica, glaciers exist at high elevations on mountains, where the snow never completely melts.

Eventually, glacial ice grows thick enough that its intense weight and the pull of gravity cause the grains of ice to deform. Under these pressures, the ice crystals slip over one another like playing cards being shuffled, and the glacier creeps forward. Friction can also help glaciers advance. Rub your hands together rapidly. Feel the heat? The friction of a glacier rubbing across the rocky land under it generates heat that melts a little of the lower surface. This meltwater lubricates the glacier, helping it slip downhill.

CREATE THE BEGINNING OF A GLACIER

To understand how glacial ice forms, follow this recipe suggested by ice expert Tony Gow.

Collect one cup of snow or if none is available use very finely shaved ice. Mix in enough ice-cold water to make the snow or shaved ice slushy. Pour this into a sandwich-size, self-sealing plastic bag. Place inside a larger self-sealing plastic bag, fill this bag with ice cubes, pour in enough water to cover the small bag, seal, and place in the refrigerator.

After twenty-four hours, run warm water into the big bag to help you remove the small bag from the ice. Take the ball of ice out of the small bag and blot the damp ice with paper towels. Then repeat the process. Seal this ice ball in a bag inside a bag filled with ice and place it overnight in the refrigerator.

Now when you remove the ice ball, take a close look at it. This ice is similar to firn, the material that builds up into a glacier. In nature, firn is tightly packed-together snow that develops when fresh, fluffy snow is compacted. The air between the snowflakes is pushed out, and the crystals become round ice grains that bond together. Water flowing into any remaining spaces between the ice grains helps speed up the compaction process.

Glacial ice forms when firn is compacted still more by the weight of snow piling up on top of it. Any remaining air is trapped as tiny bubbles in solid ice. Glacial ice doesn't form quickly. In fact, it may take more than a thousand years for snow to be transformed into glacial ice.

THEY'RE INVESTIGATING GLACIERS ON THE MOVE

Mark Meier and his team of researchers set up camp on top of the Columbia Glacier in south central Alaska. This glacier covers an area just over 1,000 square kilometers (400 square miles) and has one long branch extending 64 kilometers (40 miles) into the Columbia Bay not far from Prince William Sound and Valdez, Alaska. Meier began studying the Columbia Glacier in the mid-1970s in order to better understand the forces that make glaciers advance and retreat. Then, in 1977, the glacier began to retreat rapidly.

The reason for this change was that in its normal cycle, the Columbia Glacier retreated just enough so that its terminus or end was no longer in shallow water. Up until then, the glacier extended through the bay and ended partly on Heather Island and partly on a submerged shoal. As long as the terminus was in shallow water, the glacier was little affected by waves and tidal action. The amount of ice that calved or broke off to form icebergs was about equal to what flowed slowly down from the mountains toward the sea. Once the glacier retreated far enough that its terminus was in deep water, though, waves and tides caused the discharge of icebergs to increase greatly.

The glacier began to retreat much faster. This event was particularly exciting because Meier had predicted the onset and rate of disintegration with computer models. It also made the Columbia Glacier a cause for concern because the icebergs it was discharging sometimes drifted into shipping lanes, threatening tankers carrying oil.

At present, the Columbia Glacier is retreating at a rate of about 15 to 18 meters (50 to 60 feet) per day. Technology has helped Meier's crew measure this retreat. A helicopter landed two people on an ice pinnacle on the glacier, and they installed a reflector there. Then a laser-range-finding instrument was set up back at camp and programmed to switch on every fifteen minutes to measure the distance to the reflector. Analyzing this data revealed how quickly the glacier was retreating.

Meier's study of the Columbia Glacier's retreat is being closely watched by scientists around the world. Glaciers radiate heat, helping to maintain an energy balance with the heat that's absorbed in the tropics—important for keeping Earth's climate stable. And as glaciers melt they can also raise sea levels worldwide.

OPPOSITE: See the researchers' tents atop the glacier? What a place to camp!

FIND OUT HOW GLACIERS AFFECT THE EARTH

Open the door to the refrigerator and stand in front of it with bare legs and feet. Feel the cold air? Air flowing over a glacier may cool the air as far away as a couple of kilometers.

Next, fill a paper cup half full of water and freeze it. Peel the paper back far enough to expose the surface of the ice.

Press this into a pile of sand. See how the sand grains become stuck? Rocks are plucked up this same way as a glacier slides over them. Now rub the sandy mini-glacier over a smooth, flat piece of aluminum foil. See the gouges the sand carved? Now you know how a glacier can carve grooves in a rock.

A glacier carved these grooves in the rock. How do you suppose the glacier did this?

THEY'RE USING ICE TO STUDY THE EARTH'S PAST

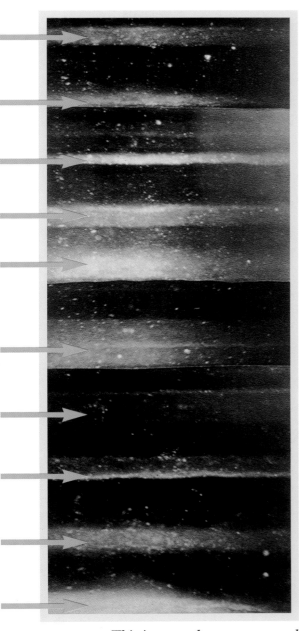

This ice core shows ten annual summer layers, pointed to by arrows, sandwiched between darker winter layers.

Scientists want to know what Earth's atmosphere was like in the past so they can compare it to today's atmosphere. But how can they collect a sample of air from hundreds of years ago? If you have ever noticed little bubbles of air in ice cubes, then you won't be surprised to learn that there are little bubbles of ancient air trapped in glacial ice. From these bubble samples, researchers have discovered that Earth's atmosphere contained a slightly different mix of carbon dioxide, methane, and other gases than it does now.

Scientists also want to know what Earth's climate was like at the Poles long ago. Ice cores, sections showing the layers of ice that built up as the ice sheets developed, provide clues. The structure of the ice reveals whether temperatures were warm or cold and whether the snowfall was heavy or light. Ice cores from Greenland are easier to study than those from Antarctica because Greenland gets several times more snow a year, so the layers of ice are thicker and easier to see.

Until recently, the only way to study ice cores was to travel to Greenland or Antarctica and set up camp. That was both expensive and difficult, so the National Ice Core Laboratory was created at the U.S. Geologic Survey's facility in Lakewood, Colorado. As you might guess, this is actually a big freezer. Researchers are issued warm, protective clothing when they check out samples.

Besides making it easier to study ice cores, the National Ice Core Laboratory also makes it possible for researchers to reexamine cores when they think of new things to investigate. And as new technology is developed, the stored ice cores will allow scientists to reconsider conclusions drawn from earlier research.

AT RIGHT: These researchers are removing an ice core.

BELOW: Here you can see some of the thousands of ice core sections stored in the National Ice Core Laboratory.

This series of aerial photos shows how waves change an iceberg. Wave erosion concentrates where there are slight irregularities. Although this flat iceberg didn't turn over, most icebergs roll, exposing new surfaces as pieces break off.

THEY'RE LEARNING TO PREDICT WHERE ICEBERGS ARE HEADING

Imagine a ship slamming into a skyscraper! That's what it's like for a ship to strike a really big iceberg.

According to Don Murphy of the International Ice Patrol, some icebergs are only the size of a large delivery truck, but an average berg is the size of a small office building. Big icebergs are as long as a city block and as tall as a twenty-story building—and that's only what's visible above water. To discover how much of an iceberg is likely to be hidden underwater, slip an ice cube into a glass of water and look at the cube through the side of the glass. You'll see that about 80 percent of the cube is underwater. Icebergs often have parts jutting out underwater, too.

Icebergs also calve—that is, break off—from the Antarctic ice cap, but the icebergs that calve from glaciers in West Greenland have been studied most closely. These are the icebergs that cause the greatest problems because they ride south on the Labrador Current through what is one of the world's busiest shipping lanes. It was just a medium-size berg that the RMS *Titanic* struck on April 15, 1912. The rock-hard ice ripped a hole in the side of the ship and it sank, killing more than fifteen hundred people. Although many other ships had already been sunk by bergs, this great loss, which included many wealthy and famous people, shocked the world. A year later, the International Ice Patrol was launched.

The patrol's service is strictly seasonal, usually lasting from February through July—from the time icebergs first begin to enter the shipping lanes until warm water and wave action eliminate the problem. During heavy ice years, patrols may continue until September.

In its early years, the International Ice Patrol attempted to get rid of potentially dangerous bergs. First, they tried bombing them, but all this did was transform big bergs into many little bergs. The smaller chunks of ice were still dangerous and they were harder for ships to spot. They also tried covering a small iceberg with lampblack, hoping this would make it absorb more of the sun's energy and melt faster. That didn't work, either. The process was very messy and the lampblack soon washed off.

Scientists decided that the best approach was to learn more about the currents carrying the icebergs. So some icebergs were marked with buoys that gave out a signal that could be monitored and tracked. Wind speed information was also collected along with salinity and temperature data—anything that could affect how an iceberg might drift. Eventually, researchers had enough information to begin to predict where an iceberg was likely to go based on its current position. Today, a computer system called the Iceberg Data Management and Prediction System (DMPS) accurately predicts an iceberg's path up to five to six days in the future. To check the DMPS's accuracy, icebergs are still periodically tagged with buoys and tracked.

Technology has also improved how icebergs are spotted. For many years, sightings could only be made by people looking out an airplane window. That limited sightings to times of clear weather. Now a special kind of radar called Side-Looking Airborne Radar (SLAR) makes it possible to detect objects in the water even when it's foggy. In 1993, a new radar system called Forward-Looking Airborne Radar (FLAR) improved data collection even more. FLAR lets the ice patrol focus on what's spotted by the side-looking radar, transforming a blip on the radar screen to a visual image. Thus it's possible to see if what's been spotted is an iceberg or a fishing boat.

This iceberg's shape was sculptured by waves and the sun's heat.

HELP ELIMINATE
DANGEROUS ICEBERGS

Is there something that could be done to eliminate potentially dangerous icebergs? Before you tackle this problem, it will help you to know more about what affects how quickly an iceberg breaks down. These activities will let you find out.

First, collect two identical glasses. Fill one with hot tap water and one with cold tap water. Place an ice cube in each glass. Use a watch with a second hand to time how long it takes ice to melt in hot water and in cold water. Repeat the test two more times and compute an average of the results. Based on this test, do you think water temperature affects how quickly icebergs break down?

Next, collect two sandwich-size, self-sealing plastic bags. Fill each bag half full of cold tap water. Put three ice cubes in each bag and seal. Set one bag in the sink. Hold the other bag and shake for thirty seconds. Then compare the size of the ice cubes in each bag. The ones in the bag you shook should look noticeably smaller. If not, shake for thirty seconds more. Based on this activity, how do you think wave action affects how quickly icebergs break down?

Now, use what you discovered while you were investigating to come up with a plan that might help the International Ice Patrol deal with potentially dangerous icebergs. Brainstorm for ten minutes, listing all the ideas you can think of. Evaluate your ideas, considering what, if anything, might keep your plan from working. Write a description of your plan. List any special equipment that would be needed. If the equipment doesn't yet exist, draw a diagram of it and briefly tell how it would work.

THEY'RE TESTING ROBOT SPACE EXPLORERS

TROV

Dante

Where on Earth could you test a robot designed to explore the moon or Mars? Jim Osborn and the team from Carnegie Mellon University in Pittsburgh, Pennsylvania, chose to test how Dante, a Remotely Operated Vehicle (ROV), would handle climbing down inside the crater of Mount Erebus, an active volcano in Antarctica. Looking as alien as a spider from another world, Dante is about 3 meters (10 feet) long and 2 meters (7 feet) wide. It has eight legs that it moves four at a time. Sensors help Dante detect obstacles and irregularities on the surface. Video cameras and a scanning laser range-finder provide information that lets the on-board computer guide Dante's moves.

For its test, Dante was supposed to collect gas samples just above the volcano's lava lake, but a communications cable broke. Even this problem was a good test. Osborn's team had to figure out how they would handle such a situation if Dante were on Mars.

Meanwhile, another robot called Telepresence-controlled Remotely Operated Vehicle (TROV) is testing other equipment that may one day be used to remotely operate vehicles on the moon or Mars. For its test, the TROV is exploring a lake in Antarctica by diving through a hole in the ice. Unlike Dante, the TROV's every move must be remotely controlled by scientists on shore. This may be done either by scientists nearby in Antarctica or by researchers that are far away and linked to the site by satellite. Even long distance,

scientists get the feel of exploring the lake bottom along with the TROV by wearing either a special helmet or special glasses. These let the researcher see the images from two forward-looking cameras mounted on the TROV. The researcher wearing the helmet can make the cameras turn, scanning to each side, by turning his or her head.

OPERATE A ROBOT

You can get a feel for what it's like to use telepresence to operate a robot helper. First, check out the terrain in your bedroom, considering the best path around any obstacles. Next, plan a task, such as making your bed. Write down a set of detailed instructions that will guide a robot through completing the task. Then ask a friend to pretend to be your robot helper. Tell your "robot" to make only the moves you order as you read through your list of instructions.

What was the hardest part about working with a robot helper? Were any instructions needed that you'd forgotten to include? Besides helping scientists in Antarctica, what kinds of jobs might a robot help people perform safely here on Earth?

How Are Scientists Learning About Life in Frozen Worlds?

THEY'RE CHECKING THE KRILL

Want to know how the animals in an ecosystem are doing? Study those animals that form the foundation of the food chain. In the southern oceans surrounding Antarctica, the number-one item on the menu for many animals, including penguins, some seals, and baleen whales, is *Euphausia superba,* or krill. Relatives of shrimp, krill get to be about the size of an adult's index finger.

Krill are strong swimmers and travel in large groups called schools or swarms, feeding on phytoplankton, or tiny plants, floating at the surface. To find swarms and estimate how many krill are in the group, researchers rely on echo sounders. These instruments, mounted on a ship's hull or towed behind it, send out sound waves. If there is a swarm of krill, the sound waves are reflected back and detected.

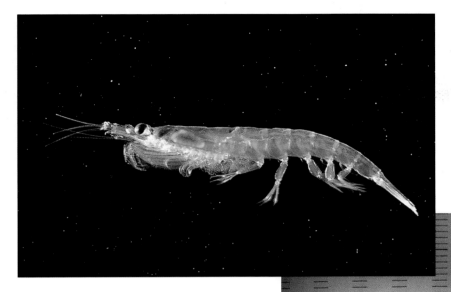

LEFT: The gut of this adult krill looks green because it's been eating phytoplankton.

RIGHT: The bars on this echogram show depth by 20-meter (about 26-foot) intervals. The wavy dark marks show swarms of krill.

The greater the number of krill massed together in the swarm, the greater the intensity of the echoes.

When a swarm is discovered, some of the krill are collected and measured. Researchers also examine the health of individual krill, count how many are females, and see how many of the females have eggs. The more females with eggs, the more the krill population is likely to increase that year.

Acoustic krill surveys have been going on for only a few years, though there have been net surveys since the 1930s. To determine how well the Antarctic krill are doing, researchers will need to continue to collect data for a number of years more and watch for trends.

OPPOSITE: This diver is catching krill larvae under the ice during the winter.

THEY'RE MONITORING PENGUIN POPULATIONS

How do you tell how well the krill population is doing if you can't easily count how many there are? That was the problem scientists faced for decades. The solution was to investigate how well krill consumers were doing. Easiest to catch and study were the penguins because they come ashore to breed and raise their chicks.

Wayne and Susan Trivelpiece decided to investigate and compare two different penguin populations—the Adelies and the Chinstraps—because these types of penguins are totally dependent on krill during Antarctic summers and nest near each other on the Antarctic peninsula.

Each year, beginning in 1976, they counted the number of penguins occupying nests with eggs right after the peak egg-laying period—November for the Adelies and early December for the Chinstraps. Several hundred nest sites were marked on a map and checked regularly to time how many days each parent stayed on the nest before going out to sea to feed. After the chicks hatched,

Each year, a thousand chicks are banded before they go out to sea.

parent birds were caught on their way back to the nest after a feeding trip to check what they had eaten.

This ongoing research revealed that through the 1970s the number of Chinstrap penguins increased while the Adelie population shrank. Since 1989, though, the numbers of both Adelies and Chinstraps have decreased. The Trivelpieces blame what's happened on warmer winters with less ice cover.

Chinstrap penguins spend most of the winter in the open sea, feeding as the opportunity arises. Adelies, on the other hand, spend most of the winter on the ice pack, diving into the water to feed during the few hours of daylight. So warmer winters with less ice-covered waters allowed the Chinstrap population to move into what had been Adelie territory. With new feeding grounds, more adult Chinstraps survived the winter and returned in good health to breed. This allowed them to raise more chicks.

Poor ice winters weren't bad just for the Adelies, though. They were bad for the krill. Unlike adult krill who have stored food and can fast for long periods, young krill need to feed all winter. Because there is very little light during the long winter months, there is very little phytoplankton growth. The best food supply is the phytoplankton that becomes trapped, building up under the ice. In winters when the sea doesn't have extensive ice cover to help collect a food supply, most of the young krill die. Eventually, this means less food for both the Chinstrap and the Adelie penguins.

This is the contents of one adult penguin's stomach. Look at all the krill!

Wayne and Susan Trivelpiece found proof in the parent penguins' stomachs that poor ice winters were affecting the whole ecosystem. After a good ice winter, the stomachs contained many young krill and some big, old ones, the survivors from the last good ice winter. There were very few krill of intermediate sizes. During the years following the good ice winter, the penguins' stomachs yielded increasingly bigger, older krill. The young krill were growing up, but no new young were surviving.

Researchers wonder if the global warming that is causing poor ice winters is a natural phase Earth is going through or the result of pollution. Wayne Trivelpiece said, "It's probably both. The bad thing is that pollution is speeding up the natural warming trend. Animals can adapt when change occurs slowly, but they may not survive such rapid change."

THEY'RE ANALYZING THE BLOOD
OF FROST-FREE FISH

Throughout most of the year the temperature of the Antarctic and Arctic Oceans is near the freezing point (−1.9°C or 27.5°F). In the shallow waters of McMurdo Sound in the Ross Sea off Antarctica, the waters are among the coldest on Earth. The water surface is likely to be covered by a layer of solid ice for as long as ten months of the year. Even below the ice, the water contains tiny ice crystals. These ice crystals could enter a fish through its gills, quickly freezing the body fluids and killing it. So it's startling that fish, such as the naked dragon fish and the Antarctic cod, are comfortably at home in these icy waters.

Arthur DeVries wanted to learn how fish survive in such icy waters. So he and his team compared the blood and other body fluids of the naked dragon fish and the Antarctic cod to that of fish living in more temperate climates. What DeVries discovered was a special substance called *glycopeptide*, which is partly composed of sugars and partly of amino acids, the building blocks of proteins. Just as antifreeze added to a car's radiator keeps

Don't worry, this naked dragon fish hiding among the ridges of ice won't freeze.

the water from turning to ice, glycopeptide keeps the fish's blood from freezing. It does this by sticking to the tiny ice crystals, which keeps them from growing large enough to be damaging. Other researchers discovered that different types of Antarctic and Arctic fishes had slightly different types of natural antifreeze. The effect was the same, though, allowing the fish's body fluids to be supercooled in the presence of ice, but not freeze.

Can you guess why it's an advantage to these fish to have developed the ability to survive where other fish can't? (Clue: Think about how this might help them compete for food and escape predators.)

HOW DOES SUGAR AFFECT FREEZING?

Find out for yourself that sugar lowers the temperature at which water freezes. You'll need two identical clear plastic cups and a cup of crushed ice. Mark one cup with a marking pen. Pour a half cup of cool tap water into each. Add two teaspoons of sugar to the marked cup and stir until the sugar dissolves. Set the cups side by side in the freezer and add four teaspoons of crushed ice to each cup. Wait ten minutes. Then add another teaspoon of ice to each cup every five minutes until you first see thin slivers of ice on the surface. As long as the solution in the cup is above the freezing point, the added ice chips will melt. Ice formation will begin as soon as the freezing point is reached for that solution. The cup of plain water should develop ice crystals first. If it doesn't, check to see if anything could be affecting the flow of cold air within the freezer and then try again. Once the cup of fresh water develops ice, continue checking and adding ice to the test cup to see how much longer it takes ice to develop on the sugar-water.

The tiny amount of ice added will not significantly dilute the sugar solution, which would alter the results. To be sure that what you observe is what's likely to happen every time, though, repeat this test two more times.

Will increasing the amount of sugar in the water lower the freezing point even more? Think about it and make a prediction. Then plan and carry out an experiment to test your prediction.

Into the Future

COUNTRIES ARE WORKING TOGETHER

Cooperation among the countries establishing research stations in Antarctica was never a serious problem. This frozen continent was not thought of as a strategic site or as a source of valuable resources. Recently, there has been a push by conservationists to make Antarctica a world park in order to ensure that this fragile environment will be protected forever.

The Arctic was another matter. During the cold war, Russia and the United States aimed missiles at each other across the Arctic. The Arctic rim countries each had their own interests in this region and resources, such as oil and gas, they wanted to exploit. Alaska's North Slope is North America's largest oil-producing area. Russia depends on the giant Siberian gas fields at Urengoi and Yamburg.

The many different native peoples of the Arctic—the Lapps or Sami of Norway, Finland, Sweden and Russia; the Inuit, Komi, and others of Alaska and Canada—united. They began to send delegates to an annual Circumpolar Conference and to actively seek laws in their respective countries that would protect their homeland. One of the first agreements reached by the Arctic rim countries was the development of a plan for dealing with oil spills in the Bering Sea and the Chukchi Sea. An International Arctic Science Committee was also established, and it has urged making the Arctic a nuclear-weapons-free zone.

Some buttercups get an early start growing under the snow.

WHAT HAPPENS TO GARBAGE?

LEFT: *For years the U.S. stations dumped garbage on the ice in Antarctica.*

RIGHT: *Finally, these ancient dumps were cleaned up and the garbage shipped back to the U.S. for disposal.*

Try this activity to find out for yourself what happens to garbage dumped in a frozen environment. You'll need two slices of bread. Sprinkle each with water and place on paper plates. Set one in a warm, dark cupboard. Put the other one in the freezer. Check the bread every couple of days until you first see fuzzy mold growing on the one in the cupboard. Is there any sign of mold on the frozen bread?

As the mold grows on the bread in the cupboard, this slice should appear to break down. Mold and bacteria help dispose of wastes in nature. Even if you keep checking for a long time, though, you won't find the frozen bread molding. Earth's frozen regions are like a freezer, preserving wastes. Arctic communities are struggling with this problem. Scientists and the increasing number of tourists that visit Antarctica each year are making a greater effort than ever before to keep this southernmost continent clean. Waste is now either burned at a high temperature or shipped off the continent for disposal.

WHAT ABOUT THE CHILDREN?

Many of the native people of the Arctic rim countries are having a cultural rebirth, providing their children with a feeling of pride. For example, in Norway, the Sami were once forced to feel inferior and encouraged to ignore their heritage. Now, children are being taught in the Sami language in state-supported schools. A Sami museum and a Sami cultural research institute have also been established.

In other Arctic rim countries, the native people are struggling for self-government, which also means greater opportunities for young people as they grow up. Members of the Siberian Inuit, called the Yup'it, have already negotiated to become partly self-governed within the new Chukotka region of the Republic of Russia.

It may surprise you to learn that there are also children living year-round on Antarctica. Their families have homes at the Chilean research station. When asked what it's like to live on this frozen continent, Andres Barros Vivanco, eleven years old, said, "I like summer best because many ships come, bringing visitors. And in the summer, we don't have to wear so much to go outside—only parkas, hats, waterproof boots, and windproof pants."

"In the winter," Paulina Alarcon Cruz, eight years old, explained, "we have to wear many layers of clothing to go outdoors, and we have to cover our whole face because it is so cold. I like living in Antarctica," Paulina adds, "but I miss my cousins and my grandparents."

In Antarctica, the children play in the snow year round.

The Future Is Yours

Now you know some of the ways people have already explored frozen worlds, what they've found, and how these discoveries are being put to use. There is still a great deal to be investigated, though. Who knows what may yet be discovered about Earth's natural cycles and the special plants and animals that have adapted to living in frozen worlds. A lot can be learned, especially by maintaining Antarctica as a unique natural laboratory.

The coldest regions remain among Earth's last frontiers. The technology making it possible for people to safely work and live where Earth is coldest is being developed even as you read this book. You can help develop the equipment and tools that will make it possible to discover even more. Or you may even want to explore these exciting icy realms yourself.

This dome, seen in the winter darkness, covers part of the base at the South Pole Station in Antarctica. Strong winds have plastered the dome with snow.

Index